Hi! I Am the New Baby

With love to Mason and Kinsey — T.P.

NOTE FROM THE PUBLISHER

When Tina Powell approached us with **Hi! I Am the New Baby** we were immediately taken with the concept of a baby speaking for a baby. What more meaningful way to remind parents and teach siblings that this baby is a special and unique person, than to let the baby do the talking. Her idea of providing a place on the cover to insert a photo of the new baby completes the personalization of the book. So the credit for this exciting story concept and the story itself goes to Tina Powell. Her creative imagery combined with her simplicity of style attract the attention of children and adults alike.

The captivating and beautiful illustrations are the work of Gary McLaughlin. Gary's characters are based on real people which makes his illustrations warm and inviting.

The combined talents of Tina Powell and Gary McLaughlin make this a book to experience and treasure. Moulin Publishing is pleased and proud to present **Hi! I Am the New Baby** as its first children's book.

Ed Boyce
March 25, 1995

Copyright © 1995 Moulin Publishing Limited
Text copyright © 1995 Tina Powell
Illustrations copyright © 1995 Gary McLaughlin

Moulin Publishing Limited
P.O. Box #560
Norval, Ontario
L0P 1K0
Canada

Canadian Cataloguing in Publication Data

Powell, Tina, 1962–
     Hi! I am the new baby

ISBN 0-9697079-3-2

1. Infants—Juvenile literature. 2. Brothers and sisters—Juvenile literature. I. McLaughlin, Gary. II. Title.

BF723.S43P69 1995   j305.23'2   C95-900419-X

Design by Heidy Lawrance Associates
Printed and bound in Hong Kong

Hi! I Am the New Baby

Story Concept
and Written by
Tina Powell

Illustrations by
Gary McLaughlin

Moulin

Hi! I am the new baby! My name is _____.
What is your name?

I was born on _____. That is my birthday.
When is your birthday? I love birthday parties.

We are going to live together. We will share the same home. What other things will we share?

You will sleep in your very own grown-up bed.

I will sleep in my very own baby bed. I sleep a lot. Zzzzzzzz. So do
not be surprised if you are asked to be quiet a lot. Shhhhhhh.

You are lucky! You get to eat good things like sandwiches and cereal and cookies. You may want to share with me. But please do not give me any. I might get sick. Or I might choke on your grown-up food.

I eat too! Well, I do not really eat. I do not have any teeth yet. I just drink lots of baby milk. What do you like to drink?

I cannot talk to you yet. But I know how to tell you I have a wet diaper. Waaaaaah! I cry. I cry when I am hungry, lonely, or scared, too. How do you sound when you cry?

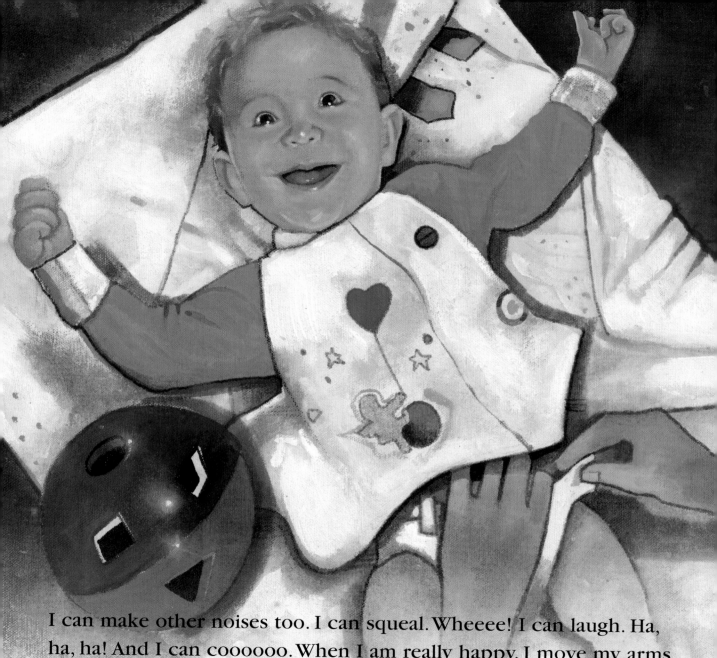

I can make other noises too. I can squeal. Wheeee! I can laugh. Ha, ha, ha! And I can coooooo. When I am really happy, I move my arms and kick my legs. What do you do when you are happy?

I cannot see very well yet. I can only see things about this far in front of my eyes.

I cannot see colours very well. I like black and white things, like toy zebras. And I like smiling faces. Your smile is one of my favourites.

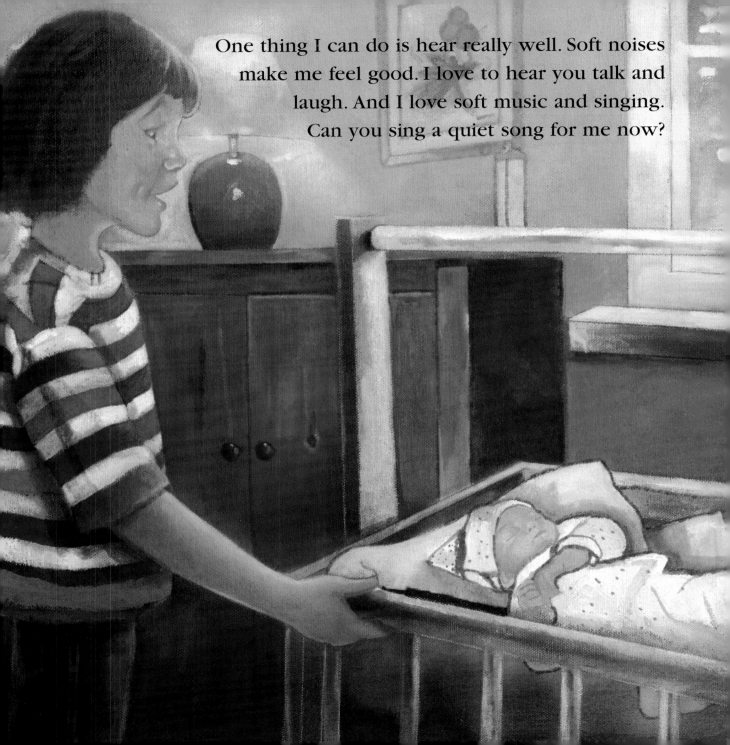

One thing I can do is hear really well. Soft noises make me feel good. I love to hear you talk and laugh. And I love soft music and singing. Can you sing a quiet song for me now?

Loud noises scare me. Can you think of some loud noises?

I guess you can see that I am very little. So, I cannot play with your big toys yet.

Please do not give me your big-kid toys. The small pieces might choke me. Or the sharp edges might cut me.

I really like to play with my baby toys. Will you play with me?

Would you gently shake a rattle for me? Would you make my puppets talk? Would you make my squeeze toys squeak, squeak? Ha, ha, ha! That makes me happy.

I love for you to read to me. I like to look at the pictures. And I like to listen to your voice. Which books are your favourites?

And I like to go for rides in my stroller.
The fresh air and sunshine feel good.
Maybe you can help Mom push me sometimes.

I like to be rocked in the big rocking chair. Rocking makes me feel sleepy and happy. Will you rock me sometimes?

I really like for people to hold me. I feel safe and warm in their arms.
Do you like to be hugged?

Sometimes you can hold me, too. I would like that. Just remember that my head and back are not very strong. You will have to hold them up for me.

Every day I am getting bigger and stronger. Soon I will be able to clap my hands, play Pat-a-cake with you and Peekaboo, too. Peekaboo! I see you!

Soon I will learn to roll from side to side. And I will learn to sit up all by myself. Can you do those things? Will you do them for me now?

One day I will be able to do
all the wonderful things you
can do. I am going to learn how
to talk and walk. And I am going to learn how to run and jump. Maybe
you can help teach me. Then we will play and have fun together!

I am really glad that I am your new baby. I love you already.